Before Paris

a novella

A Prequel to Paris, Rue des Martyrs

ADRIA J. CIMINO

velvet morning
press

Published by Velvet Morning Press

Copyright © 2015 by Adria J. Cimino

ISBN-13: 978-0692418772
ISBN-10: 0692418776

Cover design by Ellen Meyer and Vicki Lesage
Author photo by Didier Quémener

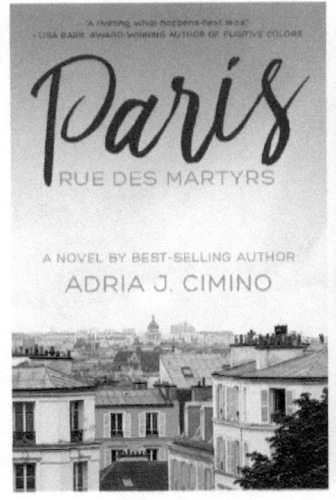

Hesitation

Rafael Mendez' eyes locked with those of his father as they sat opposite each other at the café table. A power struggle that quickly left Rafael defeated, his gaze lowered to the cup of bitter coffee in his hands. How was it that Diego still had such power over him, over everyone? At 22, Rafael was a tall, well-built man and a college graduate, yet as he faced those piercing dark eyes, he became a child again.

"You are ready," Diego said in the firm no-nonsense voice that meant business.

Rafael felt heat rise into his face. How to explain to his father that, no, he wasn't ready to take the reins in a risky, middle-of-the-night expedition to the Colombian emerald mines? How to explain that maybe it wasn't even the idea of readiness but more the idea that he didn't want this life as an emerald broker? How to explain that he longed to break the tradition of an obligation handed down from father to son?

He took a sip of the drink that chilled his throat

rather than warming it and glanced around as if they were like all of the others in this trendy café. The glamorous girls with short skirts and cherry-colored lips, the young men hiding behind laptops and cell phones. It was a place where things were happening, and Rafael knew that's what his father liked about it: He liked movement, intensity, noise. Right around the corner from his downtown office, he would come here for what he considered to be casual meetings.

Rafael liked the place for its cheerfulness, the warmth of its yellow walls that soothed his spirit even when the fog rolled in.

"Why can't you accept things the way they are?" his father hissed. "We have a good life, Rafael. It could be so easy for you."

But it wasn't good. At least not in Rafael's eyes. He didn't care about the money or prestige. He was tired of looking over his shoulder.

The Mendez family had been in the emerald business for generations. As *comisionistas*, they bought stones directly from the mines, shaped and polished them into perfection, and resold them to the world's biggest buyers. Diego was a tough, yet honorable, businessman, as was his father before him. Although he was respected by most, this respect didn't protect him from the dangers of those who were filled with greed and void of integrity.

Sometimes, Rafael had the feeling this danger—simply part of the job—was also part of the excitement for his father. The thought made him cringe. He squeezed his eyes shut, dreaming of a life far, far away and then snapped back to reality at the sound of his father's voice.

"So what do you say?" Diego asked, his eyes narrowing as he leaned closer to his son. Rafael could smell the acrid scent of coffee mixed with nicotine. He ran his hands through the thick black hair that fell over his brow, delaying his response a few more seconds. Diego was running out of patience. Rafael could feel it.

"Papa, I don't want to disappoint you, but I can't lead this trip. I can't go it alone." The words came tumbling out. "No matter what you say, I'm not ready for this." He didn't say, "I don't think I ever will be," but those were the words that followed in his mind.

Diego's hardened gaze didn't leave him. Slowly, he rose and shook his head. Then, wordlessly, he dropped a handful of bills on the table and walked out the door.

The light, the beauty of the café, suddenly dimmed. Rafael rose from his seat and followed his father's footsteps.

৩৵৵

Rafael's mother was gardening when he got home. He gazed at her beyond the patio, tending to the flowers on this exceptionally warm day. Her thin, white tunic billowed around her, giving her the look of a fairy flitting from plant to plant. Rafael didn't have to say a word or take a step for Tina to sense his presence and turn around. They shared an instinctive sort of communication. *She is my mother*, he said to himself between gritted teeth. He didn't want to think of Diego's vague comments about his past, their past. Those comments that would simmer in his 10-year-old brain until he banished them, hopefully forever.

"C'mon out here, Rafael," she said, extending a graceful arm toward the picnic table and two tall drinks. "See? I had a feeling you would be back soon so I prepared a glass for you too."

Tina's colorful concoction: cool sparkling water with chunks of strawberry and peach scattered at the bottom.

"Diego didn't come back, did he?" Rafael asked, but he already knew the answer. His father rarely came home midday. Most of his hours were spent in the office downtown—even the day before a run to the emerald mines.

Although Rafael would never directly call his father by his first name, he always did so when speaking with others about him. It reflected the distance between the young man and his father. It wasn't that Rafael didn't love or respect his father; he did, with every ounce of strength in his being. But he couldn't say he felt close to him or could identify with him. They were so different: the calm, even-tempered Rafael and the energetic, hot-tempered Diego.

Tina shook her head and settled onto a lounge chair with her drink. Rafael sat facing her and swirled a long spoon around in his icy glass. He scooped up a bit of strawberry, and as he bit into it, felt the bittersweet acidity burst in his mouth. To a bystander the picture would look so tranquil, yet Rafael knew this sense of calm was all an illusion.

"What did he say?" Tina asked in the smooth, melodious voice that would charm the birds from the trees or the best emeralds from the miners.

"The usual," Rafael said with a shrug. "He doesn't understand, Mom. He never will."

"Are you coming tonight?"

"I told him I would come along. But I won't lead. I won't go it alone, just you and me. I stood up to him about that." Rafael suddenly felt proud of himself. Sure, he hadn't pronounced the words he really wanted to say, but at least he didn't bow down to all of his father's demands.

"Did he cancel the trip?"

"He didn't say one way or the other. And then he walked out."

"We'll see," Tina said, tracing designs along the side of her glass. "We'll be ready in either case. We've been through this routine before."

"The problem is he wants what he *thinks* is best for me, but it isn't necessarily what *is* best for me."

"Typical Diego." Tina smiled and shook her head. Then she leaned forward and took Rafael by the hand. "You don't have to do this, Rafael. You have a choice, and your father and I both know that and respect that. Sure, he grumbles and complains and walks out the door. But if you don't come, if you abandon the emerald business entirely, what do you think will happen? Diego will mope for a few weeks, perhaps, but then he'll accept it and live with it."

Rafael knew his mother was right, but he couldn't bring himself to cut things off so abruptly, to disappoint his father so harshly. He wanted to at least make him proud, show him that he could be part of the family business maybe for a few years, and then somehow, slowly transition his way out. Even in Rafael's mind, this scenario seemed simplistic and naïve, but it still comforted him at times when the problem came to a head.

Tina and Diego were the perfect pair, naturals in the world of emeralds. On those trips to the mines, Tina was there to make the best deals with the men who called her "the diva." After more than 20 years in the business, she knew her stuff. Diego was there to examine the stones with those keen, dark eyes that could turn from angelic to diabolic in minutes. He carried a 9-millimeter pistol and wasn't afraid of using it.

Rafael became part of this world at age 16, when Diego announced that his only son would carry on the legacy. But instead of dropping out like his father, Rafael finished high school and went on to college. With the experience and a degree from business school, he would have everything he needed to make it in today's emerald world, his father had said.

Yet Rafael didn't feel the passion his parents had for this business.

Rafael pushed aside the thoughts and distractions running through his mind and gazed into his mother's eyes. She looked beautiful, natural without the layers of makeup she wore to the mines or for professional meetings.

"Thanks, Mom," he whispered. "But I'm going this time. Not just the two of us, but if Diego decides to go through with it, I'll be along. Promise you won't forget me?" Rafael could get so absorbed in a book at the other end of the house that he wouldn't even notice his parents' departure.

Tina smiled and nodded.

"Now go on, don't sit around with me all day! There are better things for a young man to do in Bogotá!"

ॐॐ

Rafael slipped through the house, elegant with its collection of valuable art and plush furnishings, and out the front door. He hopped into the Jeep his father had bought him for his birthday and drove back to the center of town.

But Rafael's desperate search for activity was fruitless. His on-again off-again girlfriend, Holly, wasn't home, his soccer friends had other plans, and he didn't feel like going to the university library. He was considering continuing his studies, and as he spent more and more time at the library, the option seemed more and more likely.

But today, the library didn't feel right.

As he was sitting there, tapping his fingers in deliberation, his phone rang. A foreign number he didn't recognize—but a voice that he did.

"Tigo!" His best friend, who had left to travel the

globe. He, too, was from a family of emerald brokers. The two young men understood each other, felt the same disconnect from the business of their fathers.

"So when are you coming back?" Rafael asked.

He could hear Tigo's laugh on the other end of the line.

"What's there to come back to, Raf?"

"You're still living the good life then?" Rafael hid the wistfulness he felt creeping into his voice. Maybe a trip around the world was what he needed. Maybe he should have left with Tigo in the first place.

"The ladies, the parties, white sand beaches... Everything I love, Raf! You should have come with me, you know." It was as if he had read Rafael's mind.

Then Rafael reminded himself that if he had left at the time, he wouldn't have completed his studies, and if he left now, he wouldn't be able to consider grad school—at least not for a while. He didn't want to make a hasty decision. And he knew if he did indeed follow his friend, he would end up following him from party to party. That wasn't exactly Rafael's cup of tea. So he changed the subject.

"It's been ages, Tigo. I tried calling, but it's obvious you changed phones."

"Sorry, Raf, the phone got stolen, I got distracted... and finally realized I'd better get my act together and call you."

"Well, nothing much is new here."

"You still haven't made the decision to leave that life, Raf, and explore the world?"

"You called to convince me?"

"I guess I did. I mean, I want what's best for you, man. You just don't seem yourself. I can tell by a few words. I know you, Raf."

Rafael sighed.

"I'm not going to deny it."

"Look, I can't stay on long, but I want to tell you there are better things out there, Raf. Follow your heart."

Adrenalin

"Rafael! Wake up!" Tina's urgent whisper roused Rafael, and he leaped to attention. A streak of moonlight illuminated his desk, and on the floor lay a dog-eared book. But any memories of the storyline or the fatigue that led him to press his cheek against the cool wood were unimportant. Tina didn't have to say another word. They had a mission to accomplish.

Gone were all thoughts of the day's dispute and Diego's absence at the dinner table, set early in case of a last-minute trip for emeralds. Rafael had learned long ago that the details of daily life and concerns had to be left behind when one prepared an expedition to the mines.

"You can't be distracted by goddamn useless conversation when so much is at stake!" Diego had hissed into his ear many years ago. "One second of inattention can be fatal—and I'm not just talking physical. If you lose your status at the mines, you're done for!"

These thoughts rushed through Rafael's mind as he

pulled on a sweater and a hoodie over the top. It would be cold and damp in the night. Moments later, he and Tina hurried out the door to the SUV awaiting them. The engine hummed as impatiently as Diego's fingers tapped against the steering wheel.

ॐ

Darkness engulfed the Ford Explorer as it plunged into the depths of the forest. It was an eight-hour drive turned into six with Diego at the wheel. Rafael was used to the long, gut-twisting ride out to the mines, but that didn't mean he liked it. On the rare occasion when Rafael would complain, Diego would shake his head and say, "This trip is exhilarating, Raf! It's the perfect way to prepare for our dealings at the mines, to charge our batteries. A steady drive along a highway—now that's boring!"

Rafael could only wish they were speeding along a smooth, evenly paved highway, and one that would take them far from their actual destination. But, at this point, there was no turning back.

Instinctively, Rafael touched the front pocket of his jeans, where he had a wad of hundred dollar bills totaling 10,000 dollars. He glanced at his mother, and she smiled at him reassuringly with glamorously drawn fuchsia lips. She always told him she had to sparkle just as much as the emeralds. While the drive energized Diego, it seemed to relax Tina.

The truck bumped along through the underbrush. Humidity and the damp smell of greenery seeped in through the window that Tina always cracked open a few centimeters. Rafael took a deep breath. He had accepted his fate with a solemn sense of responsibility. He couldn't disappoint his father.

Again, he brushed his hand along the pocket hiding

more cash than most 22-year-olds ever see. He closed his eyes. He wanted to doze off. It had to be past 1 o'clock in the morning. They would soon arrive at their destination.

They would stop at a little guest house near the mines and that is where they would spend the rest of the night before the break-of-dawn dealings began. Diego would fall into a deep slumber, snoring loudly, while Tina would sit at the desk all night to catch up on bookkeeping. Tina didn't require much sleep, yet always looked fresh and bright. Rafael, like Tina, wasn't a big fan of sleep either. In the next room, he would toss and turn until the first hint of sunlight shimmered from the layer of gray clouds beyond.

A flash of light, then a popping noise broke through the rhythmic humming of the motor. Rafael felt his heart leap. The Explorer spun out of control. He reached forward clutching the blood-stained denim jacket as Diego fell into his arms. The truck had jolted to a halt along with the rest of Rafael's world.

"Go!" Diego hissed. "Get out of here… You have to find Carmen…"

Rafael remained frozen in horror as he watched his mother's slim silhouette slump like crumpled silk. The windshield was riddled with bullets. But no one came to finish off the job. Diego breathed raggedly for a few moments, struggling for that once rich-sounding voice, but Rafael couldn't understand the final words his father tried to pronounce.

He hid his face so that Diego never would see his adult son cry.

The words of his father echoed in Rafael's head. He had to escape. He pushed the door open and jumped into the spindly branches that scraped his bare arms. And then he ran. So close. They were so close to the village. He could almost sense it.

A few more shots rang out in the distance as Rafael continued. He felt nothing, thought nothing, as his legs carried him through the underbrush. Like an empty shell, powered by the energy of those fatal gunshots, he continued until he fell into the arms of an old man, who brought him in from the cold.

The next thing Rafael could remember was a rural police station and questions he couldn't answer.

"He's in shock—it's normal," he heard one officer say.

"Bodies found, a male and female approximately forty years of age. Criminal activity is rampant in the area… Yes, they were clearly emerald brokers. Think this is related to the troubles over there lately?" The voices droned on, but Rafael was no longer hearing them. Officers handed him numerous cups of water throughout the day, and he drank silently, only nodding his head now and again in acknowledgement of their efforts.

Rafael half listened to the commentary around him. It didn't take an investigator to figure out what had happened. Diego had plenty of enemies, those who were jealous of his dominance at the mines and the dealings that had built his business and reputation. Yet, all of these years, even as danger surrounded his family, even as he intensely felt the fear, Rafael never really faced the fact that, yes, this could happen, this would happen.

"Do you have family in the area?" one of the officers finally asked, kneeling at Rafael's side. "We can take you there…"

"No," Rafael said, standing up on legs that wobbled like jelly. "I'm ready to go home." His voice was firm, decisive.

"We'll get someone to escort you," the officer said.

But Rafael was no longer listening.

Fury

Rafael's hands shook as he deactivated the alarm, inserted the key in the lock and slipped into the house in the dark of night. He didn't need the moon's help to illuminate the place he knew by heart. In a quiet rage, he moved from room to room, tearing open desk drawers and cabinets—anywhere there might be a clue, a document, a letter, a threat. Had Diego and Tina been warned? Had they seen this coming but didn't want to worry their son?

He searched, without really knowing or understanding what he was seeking. Yet the physical nature of it—throwing objects left and right, upsetting stacks of papers, listening to the crack of useless vases as they fell—was soothing in a way.

Rafael's anger was of the sort that came of frustration and helplessness. It had no target, other than the general nature of the emerald business itself. He didn't expect the police to find his parents' killer using typical investigation techniques. What would they do? Dust the underbrush for fingerprints? In any case, the assassin could be anyone who feared or resented Diego, and most of the people who fit that description were pretty savvy.

Time wore on, and the mess mounted, traveled from room to room in Rafael's wake. He didn't cry, didn't think, didn't talk to himself. He simply continued on as if only this hope of finding something yet to be specified could make a difference.

And then, as the sun rose from its foggy bed, slicing across the sky, a yellowed postcard caught his eye. The lights of the Champs-Elysées on one side and sloping handwriting on the other. He narrowed his eyes to read the tattered card, and it was then that Diego's final words came back to him: "You have to find Carmen."

This postcard mentioned someone named Carmen. And apparently, she was in Paris.

The ringing of the doorbell startled Rafael, breaking him from the discovery that he let float to the ground as he ran to the door.

He peered through the small window above and saw a police car out front. Hastily, he fiddled with the lock, and moments later, two officers stood with him in the hallway.

"We're making progress on the case, but we have some questions for you," one of them said. "There's no time to lose in this sort of situation."

Rafael nodded and led them into the sitting room as he made ridiculous excuses for the general disorder of the usually well-kept house.

"Did you find any clues in your search?" the second officer asked Rafael, indicating the piles of papers on the floor.

Rafael felt his cheeks go hot. He had been silly to think he could fool them.

"Nothing," he whispered, hoping to save face by being honest from this point forward.

The interrogation went on and on, and Rafael's sense of powerlessness only grew as each question seemed to lead to another. They far outnumbered the answers.

By the time the investigators had finished, the sun was high in the sky. It was an unusually warm summer in Bogotá.

∽✍

Holly clung to him on the front lawn as day turned to night.

"Rafael, why didn't you come right over?" she whispered, her breath hot on his neck in the cool evening air. "You shouldn't have been alone here like this! I would have cut class, you know that..."

Rafael buried his face in her long blond hair. He had waited to call her. As a matter of fact, he hadn't even called her. He'd sent a text message. He couldn't bring himself to actually say the words, "My parents have been killed." Murdered in cold blood. Even writing it was terrible, plunging him back into the grisly scene.

In 20 minutes, Holly was there by his side. Tears fell from her eyes, leaving wet spots on his shirt. He led her into the house, and they curled up together on the loveseat in the living room. Tonight, they wouldn't be going to his room or back to her place.

Holly wanted to know everything, but what was there to tell? The story was so brief, so lacking in detail.

"You don't have any more information?" she asked.

He shook his head.

Holly knit her brow, and Rafael could guess what she was thinking.

"Back home in Vermont, things like this don't happen, do they?" he said.

She blushed and lowered her eyes.

"It's not that... You know there is plenty of crime

everywhere! It's just that I'm worried about you… I was going to ask if you want to stay with us, with my roommate and me?"

"There's no need to worry, Holly. They got what they were after. I'll be fine here. But thanks."

Today, Holly was the on-again girlfriend, warm and lovely in his arms. He forgot about their diverging paths; she was planning to return to the U.S., and he was certain he would not be accompanying her. They had broken up in the past to protect themselves from the sad, inevitable good-bye. But then a look, an encounter, and they were back in each other's arms.

And right at that moment, he was grateful. He pulled her closer, and they spent the night there, drifting asleep in the moonlight.

Aftermath

"Don't torture yourself, Rafael," his aunt Mariana said, wringing her hands. Rafael sat at her feet on the patio, his cheek against the side of the chair. His cousins, too young to understand what had recently taken place, frolicked among the plants.

A month had passed. Men had been taken into custody. Others had been set free. But in Rafael's mind, nothing had been solved, and his own future seemed uncertain.

"I should have been on the mission without him, and that would have changed everything," he said. "They were after *him*, Mariana!"

"Rafael, they would have gone after him the next time in that case. You don't think Diego would have stopped going to the mines just because you went in his place one time?" She shook her head.

"Maybe their plan wouldn't have worked if they tried it any other time," he mumbled. He got up and paced a few yards in the grass.

Mariana narrowed the dark eyes that were exactly like those of her brother.

"I know this is still fresh, but you have to move on, Rafael. You're a young man and have many years ahead of you."

Mariana told Rafael she didn't want to talk about the past. She wanted him to move forward. She wanted him to find his way, far from here if necessary.

This conversation, or variations of it, repeated itself over and over in the weeks to come, weeks of reflection for Rafael. He had finished his studies, and he no longer had the pressure to continue the family business. It would live on through Mariana's husband and a partner who easily ascended to the throne left by Diego.

Rafael's personal attachments to the city were limited. Holly didn't make the list as her departure was more and more imminent with each passing day. There were Mariana and her family, and a few casual friends. Period. Since Tigo had left, Rafael hadn't been able to forge another such friendship with anyone at the university or in his neighborhood. Running off to join Tigo—or even calling him for that matter—was out of the question; he didn't want to ruin his friend's carefree travels with his own tale of sorrow. And Rafael wasn't exactly in the mood for parties by the pool and lighthearted fun anyway.

He spent weeks wrapping up business details, matters that were awkward and unfamiliar to him. And the rest of his time, he spent running this household of one that quickly became unmanageable. As if overnight, the garden went from well-maintained to overgrown. Finally, Mariana took charge and made it her business to stop by twice a week to tend to the flowers and fruit trees. But even this bit of assistance didn't make life easier for Rafael. Even if Tina's usual housekeeper came by a couple of times a week as well, it didn't help much. The maintenance was a symptom rather than the ill itself.

The problem was Rafael felt lost. He would shake his head with irony. Now that he had the choice, had his future in his own hands, he didn't know what to do with the freedom. He had become too used to following, to depending on Diego. As much as he complained about it, it had been a comfort zone. Now, that comfort zone— the only thing tying him to this place—was gone. And one thing seemed certain: His future definitely wasn't in Diego's old stomping grounds.

"So what am I even doing here?" he asked himself and Holly as they faced each other over what likely would be their last dinner together. They had been in off-again relationship territory for the past few weeks, not due to a fight or even a disagreement. They simply were moving in opposite directions. "Holly, you're going back to the U.S., you have priorities at school… and I've had other priorities lately, family business to deal with. There's no use trying to hold together something that is destined to fall apart."

"I said you could come with me, Rafael." Holly took his hand across the table. "It might be the escape you need right now. You know I have obligations there. I have to go back to the farm, wouldn't consider living anywhere else."

Rafael and Holly shared the same poisoned inheritance: a family business that weighed on their shoulders, on their futures. Yet Holly, unlike Rafael, didn't see it as poisoned. She yearned for the day when she would run the family operation. She couldn't imagine leaving the farm, other than for travel or exchange program stints such as this one.

Rafael looked into her blue eyes, brimming with sincerity, yet he knew his feelings weren't strong enough to make him follow her. He could see himself living and working on a dairy farm just about as easily as he could see himself as a *comisionista* forever.

Holly's kindness, beauty and intelligence had been what attracted him to her, but all of this wasn't enough to hold them together. Even though he wasn't quite sure what his dream was, he knew it wouldn't meld with Holly's.

"It wouldn't work out," he murmured. "That isn't the life for me."

She looked down, but not before Rafael could see the tears welling up in her eyes.

"I know," she replied. "Maybe I should stay, but I can't…"

"No," he said firmly. "You have to do what is right for you, Holly. You would only resent me later."

"We had some good times, Rafael," she said. "And now I feel as if you need me, need someone."

"You're not supposed to be my shoulder to cry on. That wouldn't be fair to you."

"Why do you have to be so damn good, Rafael?" She shook her head. The tears had begun to leak out of her eyes. "Why can't you say something clumsy and uncouth? Then I could get mad at you."

Rafael reached out and dried her eyes with his napkin.

"Do we really want to leave off that way?" he asked.

She shook her head.

They walked along the busy street, the chill of night at their backs. Rafael would walk her to her apartment, but this time, he wouldn't go inside.

Departure

Weeks passed, months passed. Holly left, Rafael stayed. February summer switched to March autumn in Colombia. And then came August, the heart of winter, when one would dream of sunshine and warmth. Rafael, disappointed by his months of solitude and indecision, checked off another day on the calendar in his father's office.

And that is when something happened. Finally, change was in the air.

The tattered, old postcard made its way back to Rafael, somehow finding its way under his shoe as he walked through his father's freshly tidied office. That postcard from someone he once wished to forget. And the name "Carmen," written right there to remind him of Diego's last words.

Who was Carmen? And why had Diego spoken her name at that final moment?

Rafael had hoped to push everything about that horrendous night out of his mind forever, yet here was this postcard, for a second time trying to remind him.

He held the card in his hands and sank into the thick leather chair behind Diego's desk. He looked up at the photo of the three of them. He must have been about eight or nine, and he stood between his parents in front of a cluster of Tina's rose bushes. As much as Diego insisted their life was good, Rafael couldn't help but notice the carefree words were never reflected in his father's eyes. Was it simply the strain and stress of the emerald world? Or was there some missing element in his life?

Could Carmen answer that question?

Rafael pulled open the desk drawers and dug through his father's files. He had done this once before, in the weeks following the murder as he settled his parents' business. But this time, he was looking for something more, for personal clues.

Rafael didn't know who Carmen was, but from the monument on the postcard, he was certain she was in Paris. Diego traveled there from time to time to meet with jewelers and others in the industry or attend conferences. Rafael spent hours digging through documents and notebooks from his father's travels. He sifted through useless receipts, brochures and advertisements. But even as the pile of papers mounted on the desktop, he refused to be sidetracked, to doubt he would find information that would be something other than useless.

It was when his hands touched an address book that he had the feeling he was on the verge of finding answers. He flipped through pages of crossed out addresses of jewelry shops and buyers, attorneys and industry organizations. There was the address of the place Diego stayed each time he went to Paris. Rafael marked the page and continued on, marking pages left and right.

And then he saw a name—just a first name—with the address "120 Rue des Martyrs." The name was Carmen.

ॐ

Rafael packed a bag. Not one of the fancy designer suitcases Tina had bought for him, those valises that reeked of a wealth he had never earned. He no longer wanted to be part of this lifestyle. He was tired of the superficial. Instead, he stuffed some practical clothing and a few sentimental objects—a photo of his parents, a packet of old letters from his mother—into the musty suitcase of his childhood and snapped it shut. Suddenly, it was as if he couldn't spend another minute in this home, dripping with luxury and unnecessary ostentatious decorations.

He ran through the house until he reached the kitchen and the small notepad Tina had left on the counter so many months ago. He scribbled a note to his aunt Mariana:

My dear aunt,

I'm following your advice, and I'm moving forward. I have to leave. I can only move forward if I leave this place. I know we talked about you and your family coming here and living in my parents' house if I ever decided to leave... Well, you have an open invitation as of now. My mother would be happy to see you and the children enjoying the garden. And wouldn't it be nice to bring some life, some happiness, to this place?

I'll be in touch soon.

Your loving nephew,
Rafael

At the ticket counter, Rafael used the power of money for what he hoped would be the last time as he purchased a first class ticket on the next flight out. It was either that, or wait another three days, and Rafael didn't have a moment to lose. As it was, he berated himself for not taking action months ago.

Finally, Rafael knew what he had to do—and it had nothing to do with more diplomas or more time spent in the university library. There would be time for that later. Right now, he had other priorities.

Like his friend Tigo, he had to break free from this family business that didn't quite suit him. But unlike Tigo, Rafael wasn't setting off on a vague trip to discover the world. His quest was much more precise. And it started with Carmen and an address in Paris on the Rue des Martyrs.

To continue Rafael's story, pick up *Paris, Rue des Martyrs* today!

About the Author

Adria J. Cimino is an author of contemporary literary fiction and a partner in the boutique publishing house Velvet Morning Press. She lives in Paris with her husband, daughter and son.

Adria hopes you enjoyed *Before Paris!* If you did, please consider leaving a review at Amazon. Even a few sentences can help future readers decide to pick up the book.

Want more? Get Adria's short story *Flore* for free! Simply join her new release mailing list: https://bit.ly/cimino-news.

To follow Adria's latest adventures in Paris or learn about her upcoming books and writing projects, visit AdriaJCimino.com.

Adria's other books include:

A Perfumer's Secret: The quest for a stolen perfume formula awakens passion, rivalry and family secrets in the fragrant flower fields of the South of France.

Paris, Rue des Martyrs, a novel that paints an intriguing picture of the intertwining relationships of four strangers in Paris.

Close to Destiny, a magical realism novel that explores the role of destiny in life.

Paris Jungle: What does Wanda Julienne, recently back to the corporate world after maternity leave, do when faced with a glass ceiling? Fight back.

Read on for a sneak peek of *Paris, Rue des Martyrs*...

An intriguing encounter at...

Flore

Apolline has tea at Café de Flore in her chic Parisian neighborhood every week with her mother and grandmother. But today, after the teatime routine, she dares to return alone… for an intriguing encounter.

"Flore" is the first in a series of Café Life stories by Adria J. Cimino. In this volume, it is accompanied by "Love Unlocked," one of the author's stories from the anthology *That's Paris*.

Get it for free! Join Adria's new release mailing list and she'll send you a free ecopy of *Flore*: https://bit.ly/cimino-news.

Paris

RUE DES MARTYRS

A NOVEL BY BEST-SELLING AUTHOR
ADRIA J. CIMINO

Chapter 1

Rafael

Rafael Mendez arrived like a thief in the night at 120 Rue des Martyrs. He ran all the way from the train station, where he had left one small, ragtag suitcase in a rented locker. His sneakers slapped noisily along the cobblestones, then pavement, in time with his own tears and the rain falling from a grim Parisian sky.

It was as if each minute lost counted for everything in his 23-year-old life. He pushed past umbrellas that seemed to tango as they bobbed against one another, old men who chatted with no one in particular, couples laughing, and a few sidewalk café tables left behind to weather the storm.

He was nearly blind to this first vision of the city, and only looked up now and again at the street signs to reassure himself that—yes—he hadn't lost the Rue des Martyrs. And then he stopped. He pushed wet strands of long, black hair back from his face, wiped away the silly tears of that odd combination of desperation and excitement, and sank down onto a bench facing the address he had imagined all of his life in Colombia.

Now, as the rain soaked through his jeans and his gaze traveled across the street to the only lighted apartment in building 120, his mind returned home. That's where his quest began, after all. In Bogotá.

৽৵

As a child, he would play with the emeralds. That was his first memory. Not mother. Not father. Emeralds. Because that was how his life began. His father never wanted to tell Rafael that the French jewelry designer gave birth to him on a trip for those precious stones. He only said it once—grimly—shaking his head and staring at the dark sand under their feet. Rafael remembered looking up at him with widened 10-year-old eyes as they plodded along the dusty trail to where his father would buy the stones. It was Rafael's first trip there with his father, and in the young boy's mind, it became a sacred place.

But he couldn't think of that story right now or those fucking emeralds. It was over. He had to erase every memory from his mind, the images that haunted him at night.

The one remaining light in 120 snapped off, leaving the building in darkness. It would be too late. He was wasting time. His heart raced as he crossed the street between the cars that kicked up muddy water onto his jeans. He ignored the honking horns. He wanted to move forward, and all at once he wanted to travel back. Rafael was frightened. Afraid of what he might learn or might not learn. Never be afraid, his father had hissed into his ear on that first trip for emeralds.

Before he could let his worries swallow him up with

one great gulp, he pounded his fist on the heavy, brown-lacquered door that like a clamshell closed the apartments to the world. Nothing. The sound of his fist against the wood reverberated through his entire body, but no one responded. He scolded himself for his own impatience. How could he possibly have expected someone to answer that door at 11 o'clock on a Thursday night? He placed his hand softly against the handle and sighed, knowing he should leave, yet not able to abandon the glimmer of hope that his problems would be resolved in a matter of hours.

The door creaked open suddenly, and he jumped back.

"There's no need to be startled, you know. When you knock on a door like a maniac, you should expect it to open."

A wispy redhead slipped through the doorway and onto the sidewalk. She gave him a crooked grin, lit a cigarette and leaned against the cool brick.

"So," she said, blowing smoke to the sky, "who do you want to see that badly?"

Something about the young woman struck him. She wasn't beautiful, with her almost pasty complexion and skinny figure in oversized jeans, but she had an assertive air about her that was much more impressive.

"It must be pretty serious," she continued, taking a drag. "Why don't we talk about it?"

"Do you know a woman named Carmen?" Rafael asked, his voice shaking.

"No."

"Someone named Carmen lives or lived here…" he said, his words trailing off. He felt ridiculous and unprepared as he faced such inquisitive eyes.

"A lot of people have been around here," she said. "I need specifics."

"That's the problem. I don't have any."

"What have you come here for anyway?"

"Answers."

She flicked her half-smoked cigarette into the gutter and with green eyes paler than any emerald gazed up to the sky.

"What are your questions?"

A window flew open from above and a woman's voice called out: "Laurel? Laurel…"

The person who had to be Laurel pulled Rafael against her and ducked into the shadows. She grinned mischievously.

"I've got to run."

His heart skipped a beat as her hair brushed against his cheek. But he kept any flicker of sentiment in check. He didn't have time for distractions.

"Meet me back here tomorrow—same hour," Laurel whispered. "I'll see what I can find out. I have some connections…" And then she slipped away from him and into the night.

Find out what happens next… buy *Paris, Rue des Martyrs* today!

Discover more by

BEST-SELLING AUTHOR

ADRIA J. CIMINO

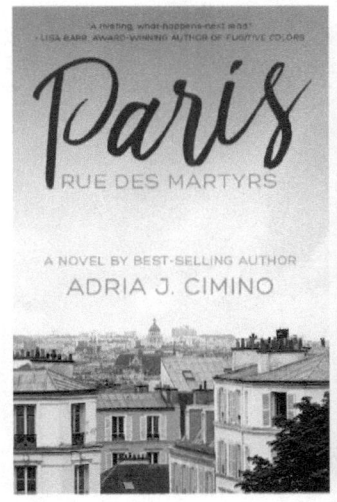

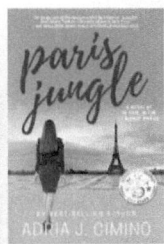

Find out about new releases and deals
by signing up for Adria's newsletter:
https://bit.ly/cimino-news

(She'll even send you *Flore* for free!)